North Ayrshire Libraries

This book is to be returned on or before
the last date stamped below.

MOST ITEMS CAN BE RENEWED BY TELEPHONE

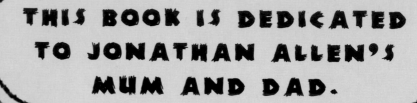

THIS BOOK IS DEDICATED TO JONATHAN ALLEN'S MUM AND DAD.

FIRST PUBLISHED IN GREAT BRITAIN IN 2006 BY BOXER BOOKS LIMITED.
WWW.BOXERBOOKS.COM

TEXT AND ILLUSTRATIONS COPYRIGHT © 2006 JONATHAN ALLEN

THE RIGHT OF JONATHAN ALLEN TO BE IDENTIFIED
AS THE AUTHOR AND ILLUSTRATOR OF THIS WORK HAS BEEN ASSERTED BY HIM
IN ACCORDANCE WITH THE COPYRIGHT, DESIGNS AND PATENTS ACT, 1988.

HARDBACK ISBN 1-905417-01-2
PAPERBACK ISBN 1-905417-02-0

PRINTED IN CHINA

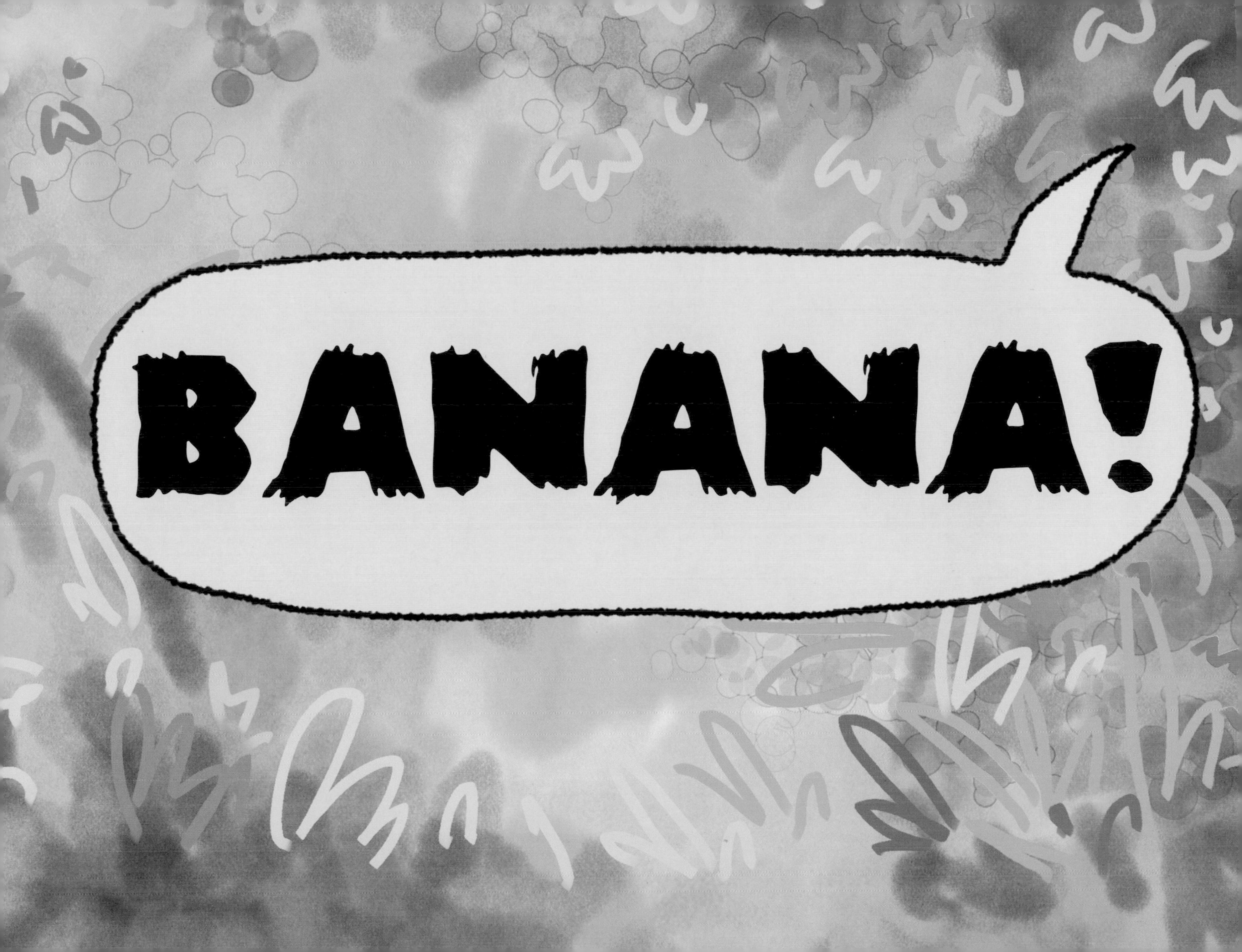
BANANA!

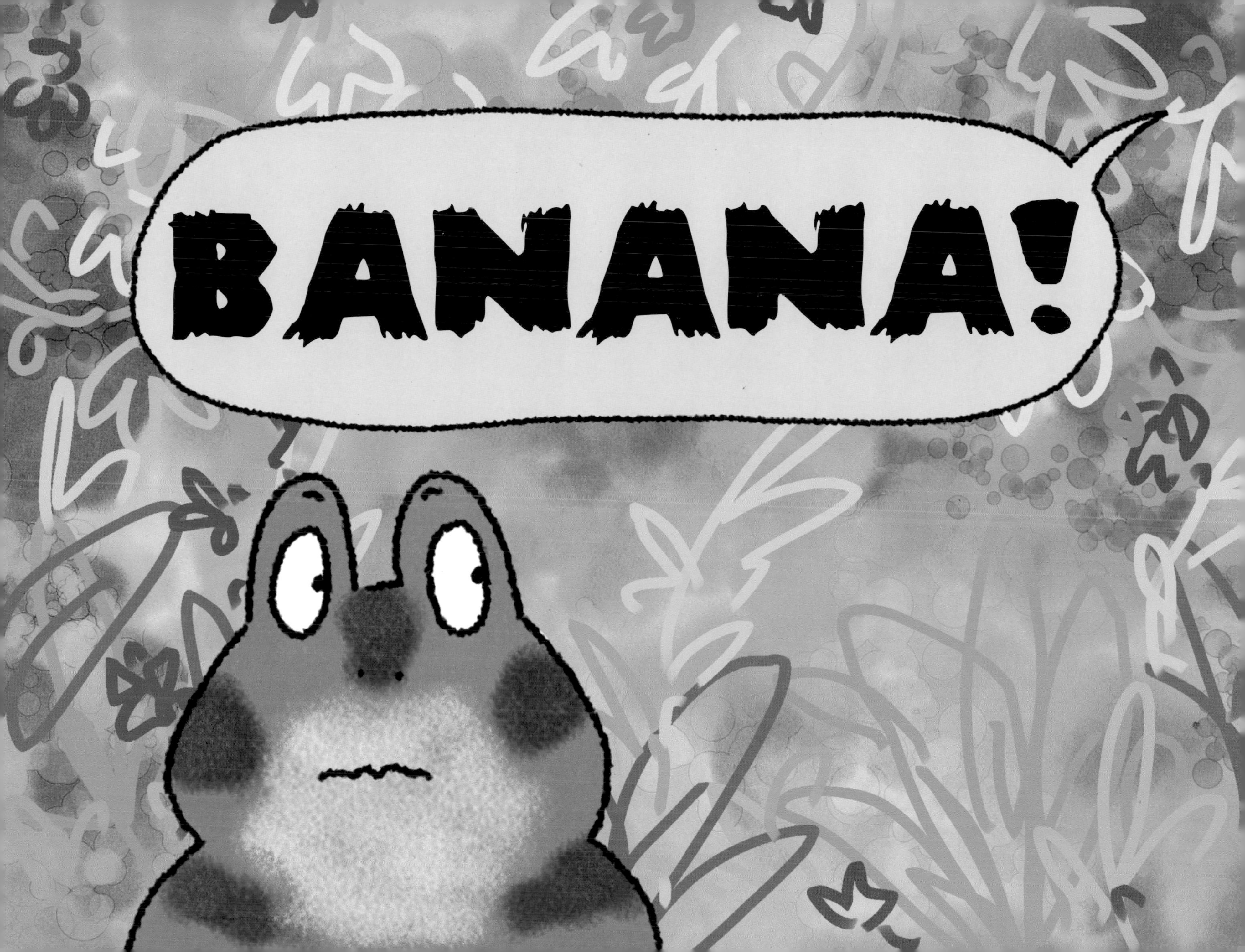
BANANA!

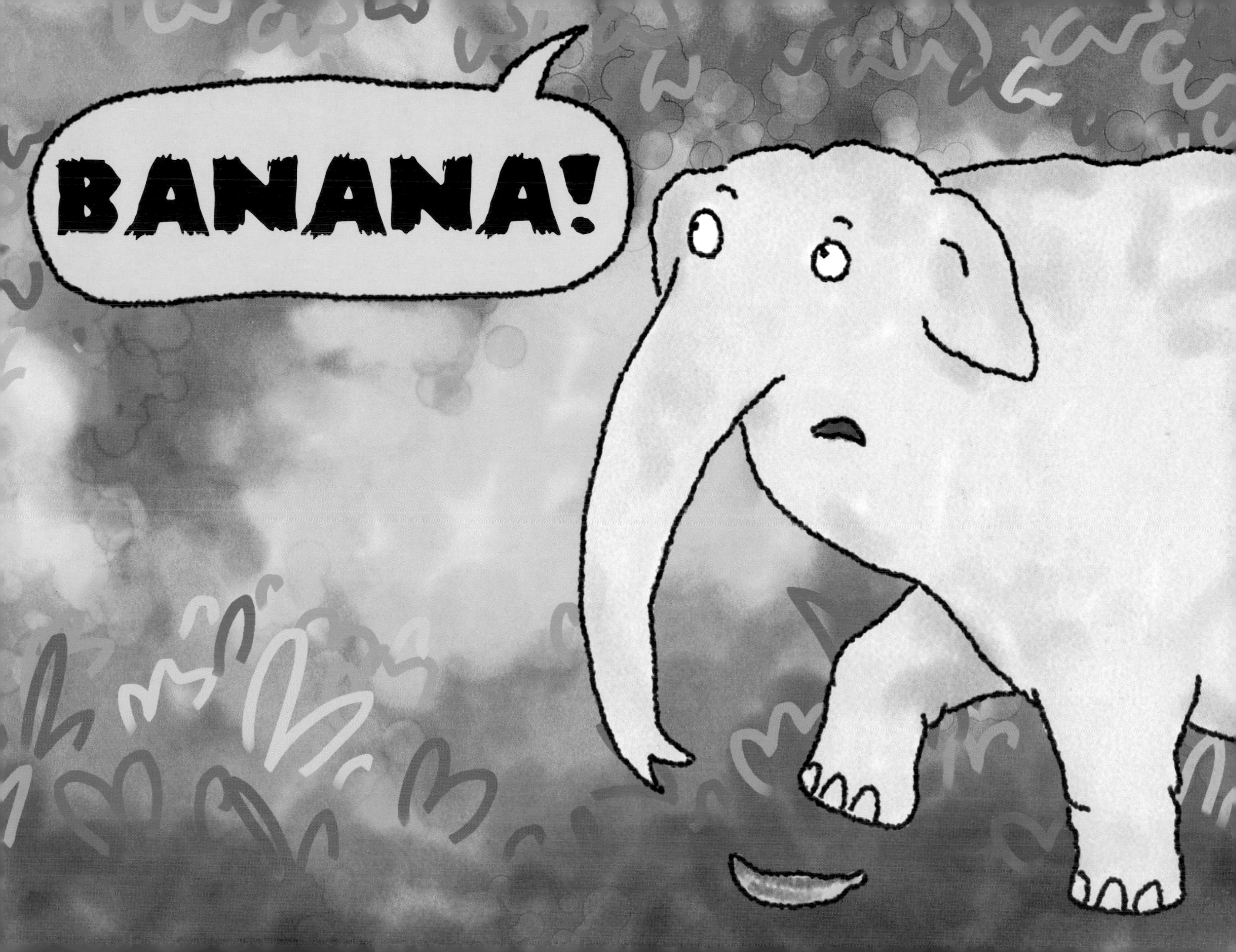
BANANA!

BOXER
BOOKS™

www.boxerbooks.com